I0815200

EID
Mubarak

DRINK
Plenty of water

I LOVE
RAMADAN

Pray!

Prayer
Time

Suhoor
Time

I can read The Holy Quran

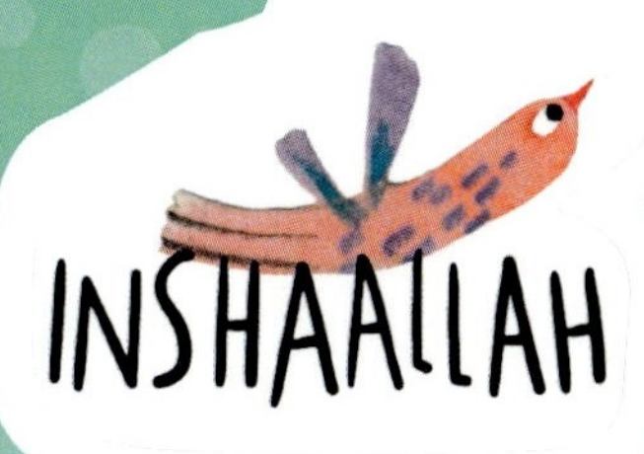
INSHAALLAH

My FIRST FAST

I
FASTED
Today

Welcome to Ramadan

Salam Alaikum and hello dear friend,

Welcome to Ramadan and your diary that will accompany you throughout this blessed month! Every detail of this diary has been tailor-made for you. Colourful duties are waiting for you on every page. One day you will meet a new recipe, another day you will write your dreams. You will draw or paint as you wish. Prayers and fasting will continue to bring you points every single day! Are you ready for the most enjoyable way to learn new things?

I wonder how many points you will collect today?

While doing all this, there is one thing we don't want you to forget. Collecting points is great fun, yet the real fun is knowing that you've done your best.

We're already so excited, so come on, let's meet on the first page!

ketebe

DAY 1

How long will you fast for today?

2 points	2 points	3 points	3 points
morning	noon	afternoon	evening

Have you prayed your salah today?

- Fajr ☐ 2 points
- Dhuhr ☐ 2 points
- Asr ☐ 2 points
- Magrib ☐ 2 points
- Isha ☐ 2 points

You have an important mission today!

You should start eating with Basmala, in iftar and suhoor.

(10 points)

3 things that I am grateful for today ♥

(10 points)

Score of the Day : /50

DAY 2

How long will you fast for today?

morning	noon	afternoon	evening
2 points	2 points	3 points	3 points

Have you prayed your salah today?

- Fajr ☐ 2 points
- Dhuhr ☐ 2 points
- Asr ☐ 2 points
- Magrib ☐ 2 points
- Isha ☐ 2 points

You have an important mission today!

Tell your mom and dad that "I love you so much!"
Note: Give them a big hug!

(10 points)

Learn a new hadith and share it with someone!

(10 points)

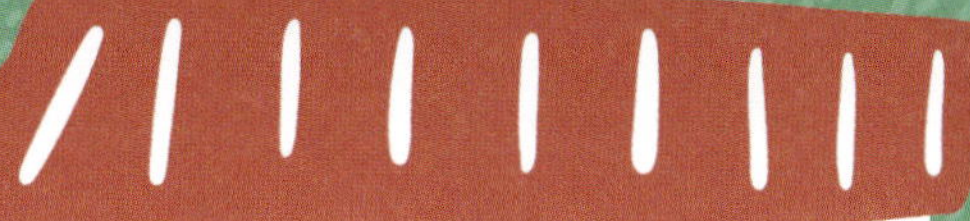

Jar of Prayers

(10 points)

Score of the Day : /50

DAY 3

How long will you fast for today?

2 points	2 points	3 points	3 points
morning	noon	afternoon	evening

Have you prayed your salah today?

- Fajr ☐ 2 points
- Dhuhr ☐ 2 points
- Asr ☐ 2 points
- Magrib ☐ 2 points
- Isha ☐ 2 points

You have an important mission today!

Give your friends a smile. Remember, "Smiling is sadaqah."

(10 points)

Research a proverb and write it down

(10 points)

write, draw, paint

FALAFEL

(Favourite Palestinian Dish)

How was yours?

(10 points)

Drink plenty of water after iftar!

Score of the Day : /50

DAY 4

How long will you fast for today?

2 points	2 points	3 points	3 points
morning	noon	afternoon	evening

Have you prayed your salah today?

Fajr	☐ 2 points
Dhuhr	☐ 2 points
Asr	☐ 2 points
Magrib	☐ 2 points
Isha	☐ 2 points

You have an important mission today!

Today, you should help to clean the suhoor table.

(10 points)

Write a salawat you know!

(10 points)

(10 points)

Score of the Day :   /50

DAY 5

How long will you fast for today?

2 points	2 points	3 points	3 points
morning	noon	afternoon	evening

Have you prayed your salah today?

- Fajr ☐ 2 points
- Dhuhr ☐ 2 points
- Asr ☐ 2 points
- Magrib ☐ 2 points
- Isha ☐ 2 points

You have an important mission today!

You have to read 10 pages today. You can decide which book to read!

(10 points)

How many words can you think of that relate to Ramadan?

(10 points)

My Dream School

(10 points)

Score of the Day : /50

DAY 6

How long will you fast for today?

2 points	2 points	3 points	3 points
morning	noon	afternoon	evening

Have you prayed your salah today?

- Fajr ☐ 2 points
- Dhuhr ☐ 2 points
- Asr ☐ 2 points
- Magrib ☐ 2 points
- Isha ☐ 2 points

You have an important mission today!

How about giving a nice gift to a loved one today? If you want, you can either buy something, make something or even give one of your own. (10 points)

Research a proverb and write it down

(10 points)

Dua List

•

•

•

•

•

(10 points)

Score of the Day : /50

DAY 7

How long will you fast for today?

2 points	2 points	3 points	3 points
morning	noon	afternoon	evening

Have you prayed your salah today?

- Fajr ☐ 2 points
- Dhuhr ☐ 2 points
- Asr ☐ 2 points
- Magrib ☐ 2 points
- Isha ☐ 2 points

You have an important mission today!

Don't forget to give salam to the uncle at the corner shop or the sister at the cashier! (10 points)

Learn a new hadith and share it with someone! (10 points)

Write or draw as you wish!

(10 points)

How you feel today?

☆☆☆☆☆

Score of the Day : /50

DAY 8

How long will you fast for today?

2 points	2 points	3 points	3 points
morning	noon	afternoon	evening

Have you prayed your salah today?

- Fajr ☐ 2 points
- Dhuhr ☐ 2 points
- Asr ☐ 2 points
- Magrib ☐ 2 points
- Isha ☐ 2 points

You have an important mission today!

You should help your parents to set up the table for iftar.

(10 points)

3 things that I am grateful for today ♥

(10 points)

My dreams

(10 points)

How you feel today?

☆☆☆☆☆

Score of the Day : /50

DAY 9

How long will you fast for today?

morning	noon	afternoon	evening
2 points	2 points	3 points	3 points

Have you prayed your salah today?

- Fajr ☐ 2 points
- Dhuhr ☐ 2 points
- Asr ☐ 2 points
- Magrib ☐ 2 points
- Isha ☐ 2 points

You have an important mission today!

You should break your fast with a date!

(10 points)

Learn a new hadith and share it with someone!

(10 points)

How about an invention you make?

(10 points)

Score of the Day : /50

DAY 10

How long will you fast for today?

morning	noon	afternoon	evening
2 points	2 points	3 points	3 points

Have you prayed your salah today?

- Fajr ☐ 2 points
- Dhuhr ☐ 2 points
- Asr ☐ 2 points
- Magrib ☐ 2 points
- Isha ☐ 2 points

You have an important mission today!

Such a great day to visit your family elders!

(10 points)

3 things that I am grateful for today ♥

(10 points)

Draw your iftar table!

(10 points)

Score of the Day : /50

DAY 11

How long will you fast for today?

2 points	2 points	3 points	3 points
morning	noon	afternoon	evening

Have you prayed your salah today?

Fajr	☐ 2 points
Dhuhr	☐ 2 points
Asr	☐ 2 points
Magrib	☐ 2 points
Isha	☐ 2 points

You have an important mission today!

Do you wash your hands before and after dinner as per sunnah?

(10 points)

Write 3 names of Allah

(10 points)

My Favourite Flowers

(10 points)

Score of the Day : /50

DAY 12

How long will you fast for today?

2 points	2 points	3 points	3 points
morning	noon	afternoon	evening

Have you prayed your salah today?

- Fajr ☐ 2 points
- Dhuhr ☐ 2 points
- Asr ☐ 2 points
- Magrib ☐ 2 points
- Isha ☐ 2 points

You have an important mission today!

Remember to drink your water in three breaths!

(10 points)

3 things that I am grateful for today ♥

(10 points)

My Recipe Corner

write, draw, paint

• LAGMAN •

(A delicious food from East Turkistan)

How was yours?

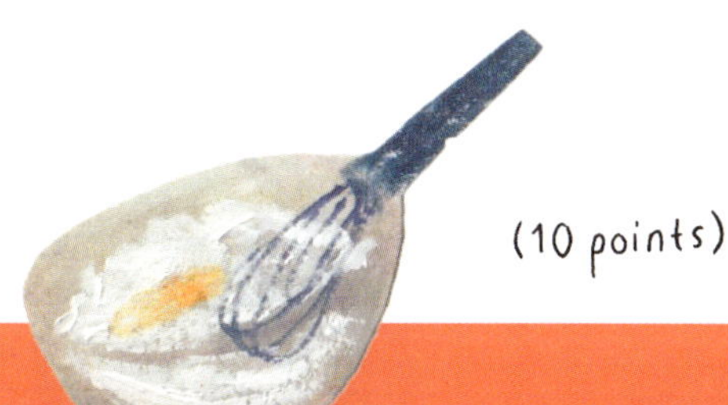

(10 points)

Score of the Day : /50

DAY 13

How long will you fast for today?

2 points	2 points	3 points	3 points
morning	noon	afternoon	evening

Have you prayed your salah today?

- Fajr ☐ 2 points
- Dhuhr ☐ 2 points
- Asr ☐ 2 points
- Magrib ☐ 2 points
- Isha ☐ 2 points

You have an important mission today!

Thank you mom and dad for the yummy foods.

(10 points)

Learn a new hadith and share it with someone!

(10 points)

Your Traditional Dress

(10 points)

Score of the Day : /50

DAY 14

How long will you fast for today?

2 points	2 points	3 points	3 points
morning	noon	afternoon	evening

Have you prayed your salah today?

- Fajr ☐ 2 points
- Dhuhr ☐ 2 points
- Asr ☐ 2 points
- Magrib ☐ 2 points
- Isha ☐ 2 points

You have an important mission today!

When you see someone doing his or her job, say, "Have a great day!"

(10 points)

3 things that I am grateful for today ♥

(10 points)

Write a story!

(10 points)

How you feel today?

☆☆☆☆☆

Score of the Day : /50

DAY 15

How long will you fast for today?

morning	noon	afternoon	evening
2 points	2 points	3 points	3 points

Have you prayed your salah today?

- Fajr ☐ 2 points
- Dhuhr ☐ 2 points
- Asr ☐ 2 points
- Magrib ☐ 2 points
- Isha ☐ 2 points

You have an important mission today!

Share some food you love with the neighbours.

(10 points)

Write 3 names of Allah

(10 points)

Write or draw as you wish!

(10 points)

SEARCH!

What does tawbah mean?

Score of the Day : /50

DAY 16

How long will you fast for today?

2 points	2 points	3 points	3 points
morning	noon	afternoon	evening

Have you prayed your salah today?

- Fajr ☐ 2 points
- Dhuhr ☐ 2 points
- Asr ☐ 2 points
- Magrib ☐ 2 points
- Isha ☐ 2 points

You have an important mission today!

Give some charity – doesn't matter how much. If you don't have money, then even a smile is charity.

(10 points)

Learn a new hadith and share it with someone!

(10 points)

JOURNAL _/_/_

(10 points)

what happened today?

SEARCH!

What does wajib mean?

Score of the Day : /50

DAY 17

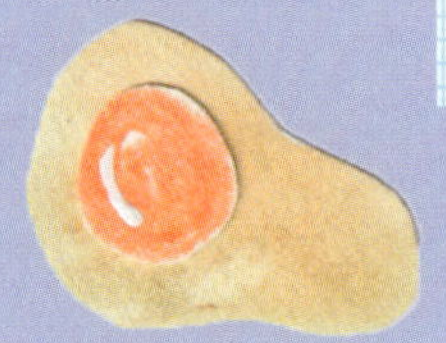

How long will you fast for today?

2 points	2 points	3 points	3 points
morning	noon	afternoon	evening

Have you prayed your salah today?

- Fajr ☐ 2 points
- Dhuhr ☐ 2 points
- Asr ☐ 2 points
- Magrib ☐ 2 points
- Isha ☐ 2 points

You have an important mission today!

Are you ready to go to school with wudu?
Why not have a go?

(10 points)

3 things that I am grateful for today ♥

(10 points)

My Ramadan Poem

(10 points)

Score of the Day : /50

DAY 18

How long will you fast for today?

2 points	2 points	3 points	3 points
morning	noon	afternoon	evening

Have you prayed your salah today?

- Fajr ☐ 2 points
- Dhuhr ☐ 2 points
- Asr ☐ 2 points
- Magrib ☐ 2 points
- Isha ☐ 2 points

You have an important mission today!

Friday is the eid of the week for Muslims. Don't forget to make the most of it by wearing new and clean clothes! From now on, you can prepare for every Friday as if you were preparing for Eid al-Fitr.

(10 points)

Write 3 names of Allah

(10 points)

What would you like to say to yourself in 10 years?

Dear ______ ,

(10 points)

How you feel today?

☆☆☆☆☆

Score of the Day :   /50

DAY 19

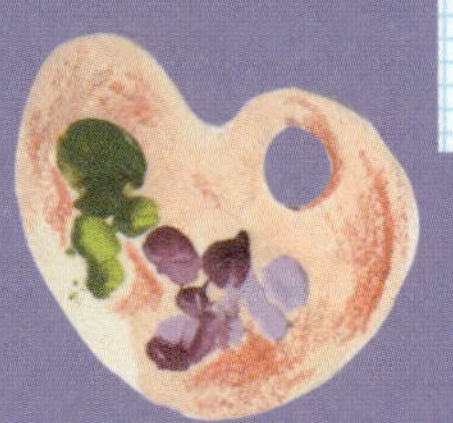

How long will you fast for today?

2 points	2 points	3 points	3 points
morning	noon	afternoon	evening

Have you prayed your salah today?

Fajr	☐ 2 points
Dhuhr	☐ 2 points
Asr	☐ 2 points
Magrib	☐ 2 points
Isha	☐ 2 points

You have an important mission today!

You can fulfil the sunnah of the Prophet (peace be upon him) by greeting everyone you meet. (10 points)

Research a country you want to visit

(10 points)

Draw your own mosque

And find your message to hang between the minarets!

(10 points)

Score of the Day :   /50

DAY 20

How long will you fast for today?

2 points	2 points	3 points	3 points
morning	noon	afternoon	evening

Have you prayed your salah today?

- Fajr ☐ 2 points
- Dhuhr ☐ 2 points
- Asr ☐ 2 points
- Magrib ☐ 2 points
- Isha ☐ 2 points

You have an important mission today!

Make a special prayer for a loved one!

(10 points)

3 things that I am grateful for today ♥

(10 points)

My Favourite Vegetables

(10 points)

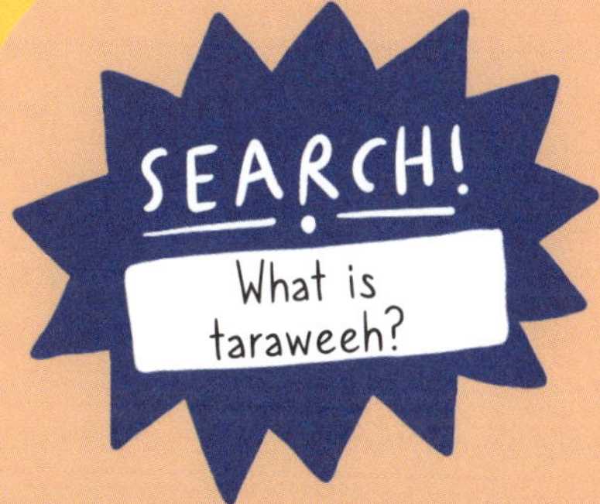

Score of the Day : /50

DAY 21

How long will you fast for today?

2 points	2 points	3 points	3 points
morning	noon	afternoon	evening

Have you prayed your salah today?

- Fajr ☐ 2 points
- Dhuhr ☐ 2 points
- Asr ☐ 2 points
- Magrib ☐ 2 points
- Isha ☐ 2 points

You have an important mission today!

The Prophet (pbuh) used to finish his dinner before he was full. Can you try to fulfil this sunnah during iftar and suhoor?

(10 points)

Learn a new hadith and share it with someone!

(10 points)

Which words or phrases do you hear a lot during Ramadan?

(10 points)

How you feel today?

☆☆☆☆☆

Score of the Day : /50

DAY 22

How long will you fast for today?

2 points	2 points	3 points	3 points
morning	noon	afternoon	evening

Have you prayed your salah today?

- Fajr ☐ 2 points
- Dhuhr ☐ 2 points
- Asr ☐ 2 points
- Magrib ☐ 2 points
- Isha ☐ 2 points

You have an important mission today!

Surprise the family and help wash up!

(10 points)

Write 3 names of Allah

(10 points)

This Ramadan;

the word I have learnt:

the films I have watched:

the books I have read:

(10 points)

Score of the Day: /50

DAY 23

How long will you fast for today?

2 points	2 points	3 points	3 points
morning	noon	afternoon	evening

Have you prayed your salah today?

- Fajr ☐ 2 points
- Dhuhr ☐ 2 points
- Asr ☐ 2 points
- Magrib ☐ 2 points
- Isha ☐ 2 points

You have an important mission today!

This time, you need to read at least 15 pages. If you say "I can read more", let see..

(10 points)

3 things that I am grateful for today ♥

(10 points)

My Recipe Corner

write, draw, paint

• TABBOULEH •

(A salad from Syrian cuisine)

How was yours?

(10 points)

Score of the Day : /50

DAY 24

How long will you fast for today?

2 points	2 points	3 points	3 points
morning	noon	afternoon	evening

Have you prayed your salah today?

- Fajr ☐ 2 points
- Dhuhr ☐ 2 points
- Asr ☐ 2 points
- Magrib ☐ 2 points
- Isha ☐ 2 points

You have an important mission today!

Make plenty of salawat during the day!

(10 points)

Learn a new hadith and share it with someone!

(10 points)

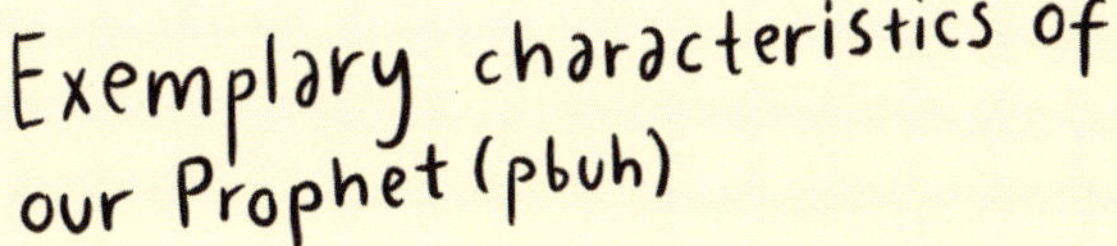

(10 points)

Score of the Day : /50

DAY 25

How long will you fast for today?

morning	noon	afternoon	evening
2 points	2 points	3 points	3 points

Have you prayed your salah today?

- Fajr ☐ 2 points
- Dhuhr ☐ 2 points
- Asr ☐ 2 points
- Magrib ☐ 2 points
- Isha ☐ 2 points

You have an important mission today!

Pray two rak'ats of Awwabin prayer immediately after maghrib!

(10 points)

Research a proverb and write it down

(10 points)

RAMADAN
KAREEM

- My Dreams -

(10 points)

Score of the Day : /50

How long will you fast for today?

morning	noon	afternoon	evening
2 points	2 points	3 points	3 points

Have you prayed your salah today?

- Fajr ☐ 2 points
- Dhuhr ☐ 2 points
- Asr ☐ 2 points
- Magrib ☐ 2 points
- Isha ☐ 2 points

You have an important mission today!

Hug a family member and tell them that you love them?

(10 points)

3 things that I am grateful for today ♥

(10 points)

(10 points)

my happiest day

:)

How you feel today?

☆☆☆☆☆

Score of the Day : /50

DAY 27

How long will you fast for today?

morning	noon	afternoon	evening
2 points	2 points	3 points	3 points

Have you prayed your salah today?

- Fajr ☐ 2 points
- Dhuhr ☐ 2 points
- Asr ☐ 2 points
- Magrib ☐ 2 points
- Isha ☐ 2 points

You have an important mission today!

Let's memorise a prayer together: "Rabbi yassir. Wa la tu'assir. Rabbi tam-mim bil khair." That is, "O My Lord, make this task easy, do not make it difficult and complete it with goodness."

(10 points)

Write 3 names of Allah

(10 points)

SEARCH!

What's the importance of Laylat ul-Qadr?

• my favourite Fruits •

(10 points)

Score of the Day : /50

DAY 28

How long will you fast for today?

2 points	2 points	3 points	3 points
morning	noon	afternoon	evening

Have you prayed your salah today?

- Fajr ☐ 2 points
- Dhuhr ☐ 2 points
- Asr ☐ 2 points
- Magrib ☐ 2 points
- Isha ☐ 2 points

You have an important mission today!

Have the Eid preparations began in your house? Come on, help your family members and collect mission points!

(10 points)

Farewell words for Ramadan

(10 points)

Write or draw as you wish!

(10 points)

Score of the Day : /50

DAY 29

How long will you fast for today?

2 points	2 points	3 points	3 points
morning	noon	afternoon	evening

Have you prayed your salah today?

- Fajr ☐ 2 points
- Dhuhr ☐ 2 points
- Asr ☐ 2 points
- Magrib ☐ 2 points
- Isha ☐ 2 points

You have an important mission today!

Today, think about all the details that make Ramadan special for you and pray to Allah to grant us all even more beautiful Ramadans!

(10 points)

3 things that I am grateful for today ♥

(10 points)

Our Holy lands

Mecca

Medina

Al Quds

(10 points)

Score of the Day : /50

DAY 30

How long will you fast for today?

2 points	2 points	3 points	3 points
morning	noon	afternoon	evening

Have you prayed your salah today?

Fajr	☐ 2 points
Dhuhr	☐ 2 points
Asr	☐ 2 points
Magrib	☐ 2 points
Isha	☐ 2 points

You have an important mission today!

No way! It is time to say goodbye... Although today is a little sad, we will wake up to a very beautiful Eid morning tomorrow. Don't forget to prepare your Eid clothes for tomorrow.

(10 points)

Learn a new hadith and share it with someone!

(10 points)

Best things which make the month of Ramadan peaceful:

Would you like to go to moonsighting with your family?

(10 points)

How you feel today?

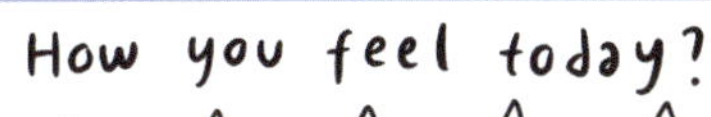

Score of the Day : /50

Eid Mubarak Everyone!

How was your Eid al-Fitr?

(write, draw, paint)

NOTES